# to Antoine

Production and copyright © 1992 Rainbow Grafics
International—Baronian Books SC, Brussels, Belgium.
English translation text copyright © 1993 by Lothrop, Lee & Shepard Books.
All rights reserved. No part of this book may be reproduced or utilized in any form or by any
means, electronic or mechanical, including photocopying and recording, or by any
information storage and retrieval system, without permission in writing from the Publisher.
Inquiries should be addressed to Lothrop, Lee & Shepard Books, a division of
William Morrow & Company, Inc., 1350 Avenue of the Americas, New York, New York 10019.
Printed in Belgium. Printed in EEC.

First Edition   1  2  3  4  5  6  7  8  9  10

Library of Congress Cataloging in Publication data was not available in time for publication
of this book, but can be obtained from the Library of Congress. ISBN 0-688-12377-5
Library of Congress Catalog Card Number: 92-54431

# Let's Pretend!

## CÉCILE BERTRAND

**Lothrop, Lee & Shepard Books** **New York**

It's four o'clock, and Jeremy
unlocks the door. Mom and Dad
are both at work, but he can hear
Booby jumping for joy on the other
side of the door.

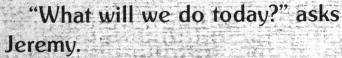

"What will we do today?" asks
Jeremy.

On Saturday the whole family will
go on their spring vacation. There
is lots to do to get ready. Jeremy
needs new swimming trunks and
sunglasses and sandals.

"I know what," he tells Booby.
"Let's pretend we're going shopping."

Booby is a little afraid of the escalator, but Jeremy holds him tight. "Good dog, Booby," he tells him.

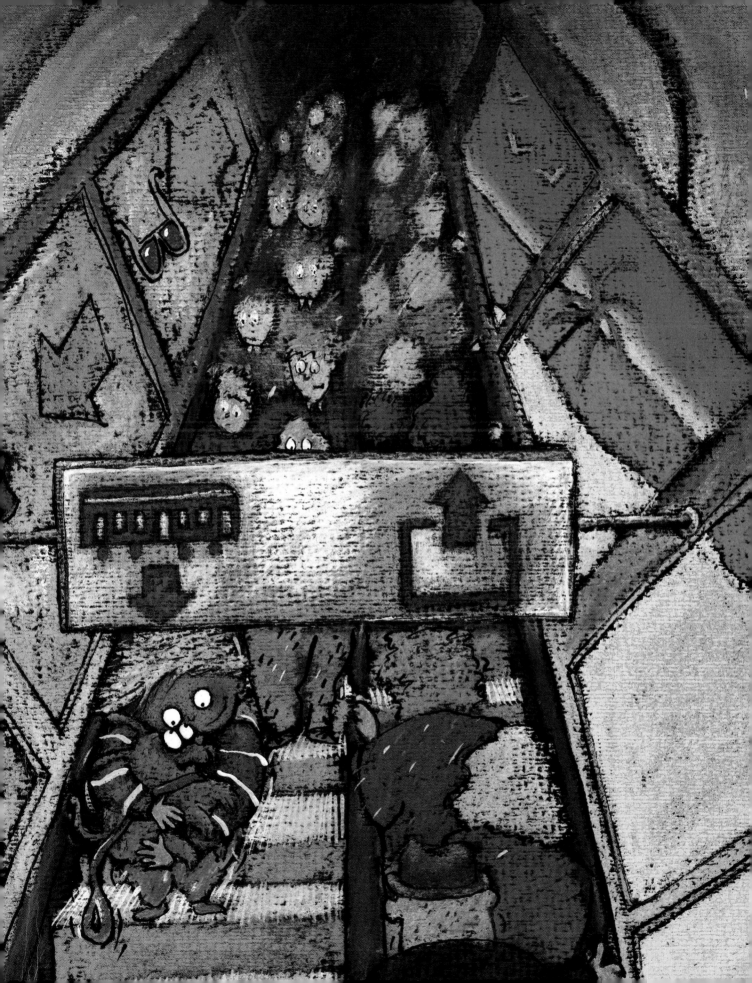

Jeremy picks out polka-dot
swimming trunks and red sandals to
match. It's a little bit embarrassing
when Booby opens the dressing
room curtain. "Bad dog, Booby!"

Now for some sunglasses.
Jeremy likes sunglasses with
flowers the best.

"Our shopping is all done now, Booby," says Jeremy. "It's time for a soda."

"Who cares if it's raining today.
It will be sunny for our vacation."

"We'll sail away to a great big city."

"The Statue of Liberty will be
happy to see us."

"Don't be afraid, Booby. The
moon will show us the way home."

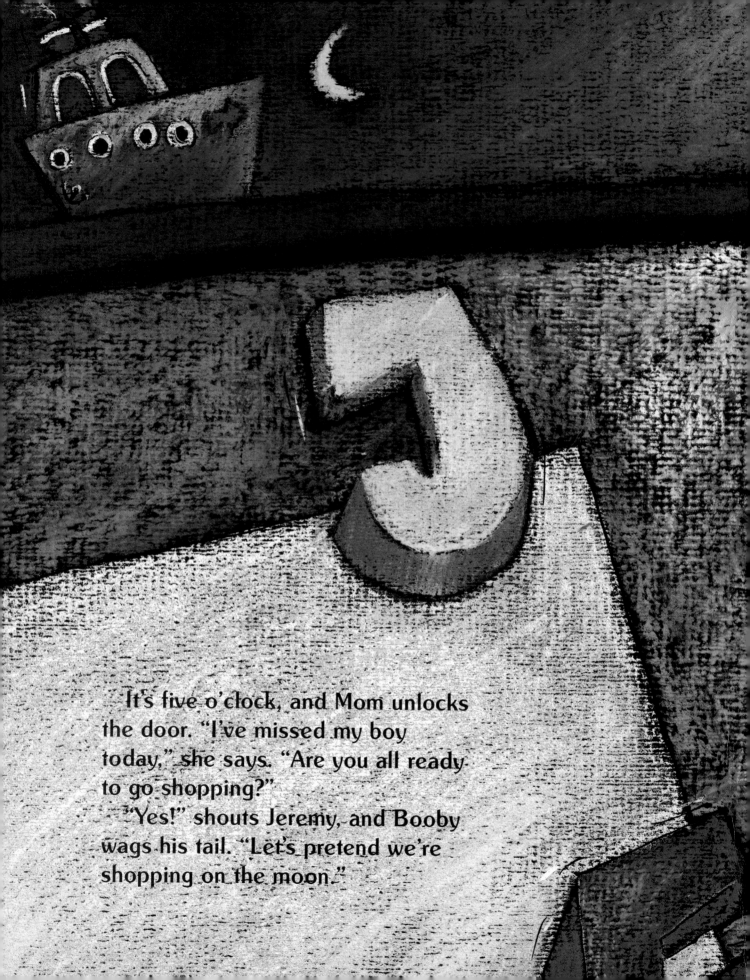

It's five o'clock, and Mom unlocks
the door. "I've missed my boy
today," she says. "Are you all ready
to go shopping?"

"Yes!" shouts Jeremy, and Booby
wags his tail. "Let's pretend we're
shopping on the moon."